# Thomas and Percy to the Rescue

**Based on *The Railway Series*
by The Rev. W. Awdry**

EGMONT

The engines were talking in the engine shed.
"Everyone seems much happier in the springtime,"
said Thomas.
"But we have to work extra hard in the springtime,"
grumbled James. "The Fat Controller makes us
travel down to the coast to work!"
"I like the salty coast air in my smokebox!" said
Percy.
"Pah! It's the countryside that gets me really fired
up!" snorted James, as he puffed away to collect
some fuel trucks from the Docks.

The Fat Controller told Thomas and Percy they would be working at the scrapyard.

"Where do you like working best?" Percy asked Thomas, as they arrived at the scrapyard.

"I don't really mind where I work," said Thomas. "So long as I can be a Really Useful Engine."

"We'll be working hard today," said Percy. "The Fat Controller said there is a large pile of scrap metal for us to move."

When Thomas and Percy shunted some trucks into a siding at the scrapyard, they saw an old coach there, looking rather sad.

"What are you doing here?" asked Percy, in surprise.

"They call me Old Slow Coach," she said. "They say I'm not useful any more, so I was sent to the scrapyard," she added, sadly.

"You are a little dusty, but you look in perfect shape to me," said Thomas, kindly.

"Excuse me," Percy's Driver said to the Yard Manager. "What will happen to this coach?"
"Old Slow Coach has been here for years," said the Yard Manager. "She's not useful any more, so she'll be broken up for scrap some time soon."
Thomas and Percy felt very sorry for the coach.
"We'll try and help you," said Thomas, but he really didn't know what they could do.

James whistled happily as he pulled the fuel trucks through the countryside. He was making good time, so he knew The Fat Controller would be pleased with him. But James did not notice that one of the trucks was leaking fuel on to the track. Suddenly, a spark flew out of James' funnel and set the leaking fuel on fire!

"HELP!" whistled James, in shock as he sped along the track with clouds of smoke and flames flying out behind him.

James moved quickly off the main track and stopped in a siding. His Driver leapt down from the cab and rushed to the emergency phone to call for help. "Hello, please send help quickly," he said. "James' trucks are on fire and they're carrying fuel, so it's very dangerous!"

The Firemen set out straight away. James waited anxiously while his Driver tried to put out the fire.

Thomas and Percy had finished working at the scrapyard. When they reached the junction, they were surprised to see smoke. A Guard was waving a red warning flag at them.

"Sparks from James' funnel have caused a fire in some fuel trucks," he told them. "It's a bit of a mess, but the Firemen have now got the fire under control."

"You said the countryside got you all fired up," Percy told James, "but I didn't think you meant it this way!"

"Pah!" snorted James. "It was the stupid trucks' fault, not mine!"

"It is safe for you to move past James now!" said the Fireman to Thomas and Percy. The engines puffed slowly past James. They felt rather sorry for him now.

Thomas and Percy went to Tidmouth Station. The Drivers talked to the Station Master and the engines had a long, cool drink at the water tower. When they had filled up their tanks, they waited for their Drivers to return. Suddenly, their Drivers came running towards them.

"Are we late for something?" asked Thomas.

"We've just heard the workmen's hut at the seaside is on fire!" said Thomas' Driver. "Let's go and see what we can do to help."

When Thomas and Percy arrived at the burning building, they saw the fire engines had already arrived. The Firemen were using hoses to fight the fire. But they had a problem, they were about to run out of water!

"We can't use sea water," said a Fireman, "because it clogs up our works. And if we can't find more water from somewhere, then I'm afraid we'll just have to let the workmen's hut burn!"

Thomas had a good idea, "Why don't you use the water in our tanks?" he said. "We've just refilled them at Tidmouth Station, so there should be plenty for you to use!"

"You're a very clever engine!" said the Chief Fireman. He called over all the Firemen and told them about Thomas' plan. The Firemen were impressed. They quickly brought their hoses to Thomas and Percy and used the water in their tanks to tackle the fire.

Thomas and Percy watched the Fireman fight the fire. They had to use nearly all the water from the engines' tanks. Unfortunately, when the smoke cleared, everyone could see the workmen's hut had been destroyed.

"Thank you all for your hard work," said the Foreman. "It's a terrible shame that the hut has burnt down. My workmen lived there and I don't know where they can stay now. Does anyone have any ideas?"

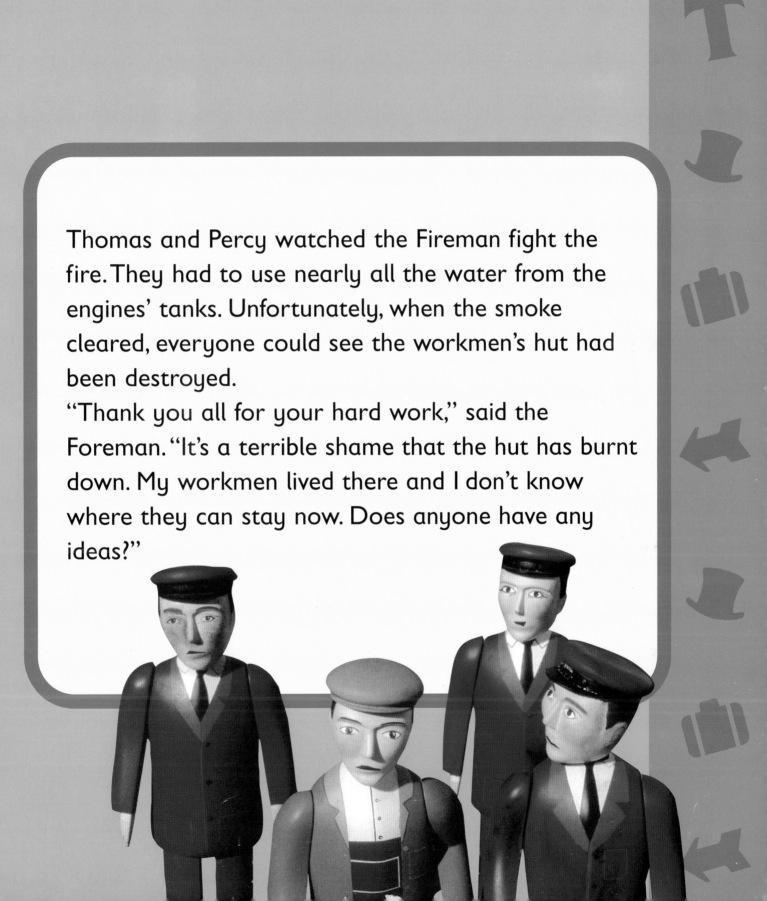

"I think I know where they can stay!" said Percy. "We can bring Old Slow Coach here for them to live in. She would be the perfect new home for the workmen!"

"She'll be really comfortable, too!" added Thomas.

"What a great idea, Percy!" said his Driver.

"I'll check The Fat Controller is happy for us to bring Old Slow Coach here," said Thomas' Driver. The Fat Controller thought it was a very good idea.

"I'll get the scrapyard Manager to clean her up, so she'll be ready for you to collect her!" he said.

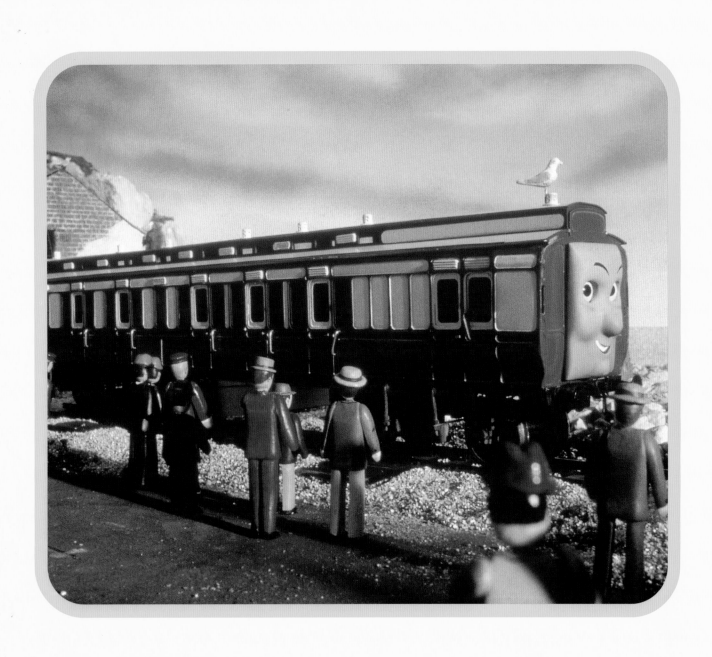

Old Slow Coach was now a very happy Coach indeed. "I can't thank you enough, I feel really splendid!" she said to Thomas and Percy, as they took her down to her new home at the seaside. When they arrived, everyone agreed there was nothing really 'Old' or 'Slow' about Coach, who would continue to be a Really Useful Coach for ever more!

First published in Great Britain 2002
by Egmont UK Limited
239 Kensington High Street, London W8 6SA
This edition published 2007

Thomas the Tank Engine & Friends™

A BRITT ALLCROFT COMPANY PRODUCTION

Based on The Railway Series by The Reverend W Awdry
© 2007 Gullane (Thomas) LLC. A HIT Entertainment Company

ISBN 978 1 4052 2975 3
ISBN 1 4052 2975 6
1 3 5 7 9 10 8 6 4 2
Printed in China